For Daniel and Eleanor, shine bright with your own special light
- Sally Pomme Clayton -

For Nazli
- Amin Hassanzadeh Sharif -

For thousands of years, people have been telling stories.
From this rich global heritage, we can find stories that are
strikingly similar but also different. *One Story, Many Voices*
explores well-known stories from all over the world.
For teacher resources and more information, visit
www.tinyowl.co.uk

The book and the accompanying music was conceived and initiated by
Dr Laudan Nooshin. The music was project-led by Soosan Lolaver.

First published in the United Kingdom and the United States in 2019
by Tiny Owl Publishing, London

A catalogue record for this book is available from the British Library.
A CIP record for this book is available from the Library of Congress.

ISBN 978-1-910328-43-9

Printed in Malta

The Phoenix of Persia

Sally Pomme Clayton

Amin Hassanzadeh Sharif

TINY OWL

Storytelling and the Shahnameh

For thousands of years, in many cultures around the world,
stories have been accompanied by music. Together, storytelling and
music can transport listeners to other worlds, other times, and other places.

Iran has an ancient tradition of storytelling and poetry where musicians play
instruments to bring stories to life. The most important epic in Iran is called the
Shahnameh (pronounced Shaah-naah-meh), which means "The Book of Kings".
It was written by the poet Abolqasem Ferdowsi who lived about a thousand
years ago. It took over 30 years to write, and has over 50,000 rhyming couplets.
The *Shahnameh* is considered to be one of the greatest epics of world literature.

The Phoenix of Persia is about a mythical bird, the Simorgh, one of the most magical
characters in the *Shahnameh*. The Simorgh takes care of a tiny baby, who grows
up to become Prince Zal – the hero of many other stories in the *Shahnameh*.

In this special edition, the story has been set to music, with each instrument
representing a different character. You can listen to music composed by
Amir Eslami (*ney*), Nilufar Habibian (*qanun*), Saeid Kord Mafi (*santur*), and
Arash Moradi (*tanbur*). You can find out more about the Iranian instruments
at the back of the book. The music accompanies Sally Pomme Clayton's
stunning narration of this classic tale from the *Shahnameh*.

Use the QR code above to play the music
or visit *www.tinyowl.co.uk/phoenixofpersia*
for further resources and information.

The children raced into Daneshjoo park. Carpets were spread on the ground, lights twinkled in the trees, and there were stalls heaped with freshly picked fruit and nuts. Ali pulled coins from his pocket and bought a tray of sweet, ripe mulberries. Shirin grabbed her brother's hand.

"Let's sit at the front!"

They wound their way through the crowd, as musicians tuned their instruments and the storyteller tested her microphone.

"What story are they going to tell?" asked Shirin, licking purple mulberry juice from her fingers.

"It's going to be epic!" said Ali. "Magic mixed with history. It's about an ancient Persian king who..."

The sound of drums echoed across the square.

"Shh! It's starting," whispered Shirin.

The storyteller began to speak.

Once upon a time … *yeki bud, yeki nabud* … far from humans and near the sun, there was a mountain made of jewels. It crunched and sparkled.

The Mountain of Gems.

At the top of the mountain was a spreading tree. Seeds hung from its branches, waiting to be born.

The Tree of All Seeds.

At the top of the tree was a giant nest. Sitting in the
nest was a bird, with curving beak and trailing tail.
Her feathers flashed, scarlet, ruby, purple, gold.
She was the size of thirty birds and shone
like a hundred suns.

The Simorgh!

The bird flapped her wings, and the
tree shook. Seeds blew, seeds flew,
seeds scattered across Earth.

Life came into being.

The Simorgh had a secret. She was a firebird!
Her feathers had magic powers. They could
grant wishes, make dreams come true.

Every thousand years the Simorgh flapped her wings
and set fire to her nest. Flames flickered, and out
of the raging fire hopped a new Simorgh,
born from the ashes.

The Simorgh swooped over the
Mountain of Gems. She had seen
worlds created, worlds destroyed.
And it had made her wise.

The Phoenix of Persia.

Ancient Persia was ruled by King Sam and Queen Aram. Their palace was magnificent. It had bronze gates and golden pillars, halls carved of stone, shady gardens, and cooling fountains. The king and queen had everything – except a child. They longed for a baby. But weeks, months, years passed, and no child came.

Then, at last, Queen Aram held a bundle wrapped in a blanket.

"We have a baby boy!" she cried.

King Sam was filled with joy.

"I name our son Zal – Prince Zal! A prince for the throne of Persia."

The king pulled back the blanket to kiss his newborn boy.

The baby was beautiful, with black eyes and rosy cheeks.
But his hair was white as snow.

"This is not the hair of a baby," said King Sam. "This is
the hair of an old man."

Queen Aram stroked the baby's head.

"We have been blessed with a son!"

"I want a perfect prince," snapped the king. "With black hair,
like my own."

"You love a snowy day," reminded the queen, "clean sheets,
a fluffy white goose feather."

King Sam's joy turned to sorrow.
    "This baby looks like a ghost, or a demon!
This is no child of mine."
The queen hugged Zal tight. But the king cried,

"This boy will bring
the kingdom doom.
He must go."

The king called a soldier
and commanded,
    "Get this monster out of here.
Take him to the mountains and
leave him."

The queen wept. But the soldier
carried Prince Zal away.

The soldier rode with the baby,
out of the kingdom,
        through the forest,
            to distant mountains.

With heavy heart, the soldier placed Prince Zal
on cold, hard rocks.
        "How can a baby survive in the wilderness?"
The soldier shook his head, and rode away.

Dusty wind blew.
A leopard prowled.
A wolf howled.
Zal began to cry.

He was hungry, and his sobs echoed
across the mountain.

Then there was a flash of red, of gold, and the fluttering of wings!

The Simorgh flew overhead, seeking food for her chicks.
She heard crying, and swooped down.
   "Poor creature! There is always room for one more."
She clasped the baby in her claws.
   "I'll take care of you."
And she soared into the sky.

The Simorgh carried Zal, over sparkling jewels, to the
Mountain of Gems. Up, up, to the Tree of All Seeds.

The Simorgh's nest smelled of sandalwood. It was full
of chicks, squeaking, opening their beaks to be fed.
The Simorgh tucked Zal into a bed of feathers.

"Something precious will grow from this seed," she said.

The chicks taught Zal to hop and chirp, and he grew strong.
But when the chicks learned how to fly, Zal was left alone.

"Now, lessons can start!" cried the Simorgh.
A thousand tiny holes appeared in her
beak. And she began to speak –
every language in the world!

The Simorgh taught Zal
poetry, science, song,
the names of plants,
how to draw, the
history of the Universe.
She had seen it all!

Zal learned to run,
to hunt, to make a fire.
"All a prince needs to know,"
said the Simorgh.

Zal watched the Simorgh swooping,
soaring, her tail dripping fire. What a mother,
what a teacher! Sixteen years passed, and Zal became wise.

"Help!" cried King Sam,
sitting up in bed.
"Not another nightmare?"
asked the queen.
"I was tumbling through
branches, twigs, seeds!"
"Sixteen years of bad dreams,"
said Queen Aram.

Sam splashed water on his face,
and caught his reflection in the mirror.
He had aged. His hair had turned
as white as snow.

"Why did I send our son away?" he wept. "There has been nothing but emptiness without him."

"Perhaps he's still alive," whispered the queen.

King Sam called the soldier.

"Do you remember where you left Prince Zal?"
The soldier bowed.

"How could I forget, Your Majesty?"

"Fetch the horses. Lead the way. I will make a memorial for our boy, and pray for his forgiveness."

King Sam and the soldier rode into the mountains.
Past leopard tracks and wolf dens.
        "How could a baby survive?" said the king.
He gathered stones, placing them in a circle
to make a grave.

When high above, he saw a young man,
leaping like a deer over the rocks.

   A radiant youth with bright, white hair.

Sam rubbed his eyes. The boy looked just like him.
        "My son!" cried the king. "You are alive!"

"Can you forgive me?" called King Sam.
"You are a precious gift I threw away. Now I know –
white hair, black hair, no hair – all life is to be treasured."

Zal bounded down the mountainside.
      "Father?"
Sam opened his arms wide.
      "Prince Zal – come home."
Zal gazed at the thick forest and towering peaks.
      "This is home," he said.

Sam took off his crown, and offered
it to his son.
      "The throne is yours."
Zal shook his head.
      "I cannot leave my mother."

Flames flickered and the Simorgh appeared!

"White hair brings wisdom," she said to Sam.
Then she turned to Zal.

"Being human is being able to forgive."
Zal held out his hands, and his father clasped them tight.
The years of misery were gone.

"All birds must fly the nest,"
said the Simorgh. "It is time for you to
go. But pluck some feathers from
my tail. If you are in trouble,
burn one, I will come."

Zal pulled sparkling
feathers from the
Simorgh's long tail,
and thanked his
phoenix mother.

Father and son set off
for home, as the Simorgh
beat giant wings, and
soared into the sky.

Queen Aram was waiting to greet them.
At last, Zal met his human mother.

"My jewel has returned!" she said.

The whole country welcomed King Zal.

"I will rule well," he cried. "And the
Simorgh will help."

Zal took a fiery feather, and placed it like wings
around his crown.

"From now on, all kings will wear
feathers on their crown!" he declared. "So everyone
is protected by *the Phoenix of Persia*."

The musicians played their final notes, and a hush came over the audience. The performers bowed, and cheers erupted.

"Did Zal burn a feather?" whispered Shirin.
"That's tomorrow's story," replied her brother.

The children jumped to their feet.
"Let's have walnuts before we go," said Ali, pulling the last
coin from his pocket. "What's this?" he said.

In the palm of his hand was an ancient coin. Worn and darkly
silver, on it was an image of a king wearing a crown –
topped with *a pair of wings*.

In the recording of *The Phoenix of Persia*, each instrument is associated with a different character in the story. Discover more about the Iranian instruments you can hear.

Ney (or nei) is an end-blown reed flute. It is used in Iranian classical music, but it has folk roots, most likely as a shepherd's pipe. It is often associated with Sufism, a mystical branch of Islam. In *The Phoenix of Persia*, the sound of the ney represents the Simorgh.

Qanun is a horizontal zither with strings in rows which are plucked with a plectrum. In *The Phoenix of Persia*, the sound of the qanun represents Prince Zal.

Tanbur is a long-necked lute with three strings which are plucked and strummed. The tanbur originally comes from the Kurdish region of western Iran. It is often used in religious rituals in Kurdistan where many regard it as a sacred instrument. In *The Phoenix of Persia*, the sound of the tanbur represents the King and Queen, and the palace.

Daff is a large, wooden frame drum, covered with a skin or synthetic head. The drum is played with the hand and fingers. It has small metal rings on the inside of the frame that jingle loudly when the drum is shaken!

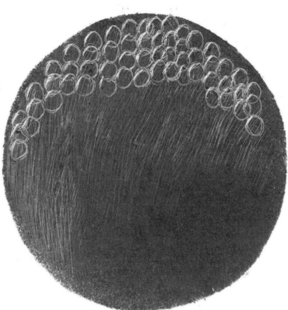

Like the tanbur, the daff originally comes from the Kurdish region of western Iran. In *The Phoenix of Persia*, the daff represents the soldier and king on their horses. It is also used in the celebrations at the end of the story.

Santur is a trapezium-shaped dulcimer played with delicate hammers which are covered with felt. It has a glittering sound and in *The Phoenix of Persia*, the santur represents the Mountain of Gems.